Wake Up, SAM!

Written by Ski Michaels
Illustrated by Diane Paterson

Troll Associates

Library of Congress Cataloging in Publication Data

———

Wake up, Sam!

Summary: Sam the bloodhound's habit of sleeping any-
where gets him into a lot of trouble.
    [1. Dogs—Fiction] I. Paterson, Diane, ill.
II. Title.
PZ7.P3656Wak   1986   [E]   85-14115
ISBN 0-8167-0580-1 (lib. bdg.)
ISBN 0-8167-0581-X (pbk.)

10   9   8   7   6   5   4   3   2   1

Wake Up, SAM!

Sleep is good. Everyone needs sleep. But Sam the bloodhound slept too much. He was always sleeping.

Why was Sam so sleepy? Was he
a bloodhound with tired blood?
Was he a lazy hound dog?

No! Sam did not have tired blood. He was not a lazy hound dog. Sam needed a good reason to stay awake. If he did not have a good reason, he slept. And Sam slept a lot.

Sam slept here. He slept there.
He slept anywhere he could.
Sleeping everywhere made lots
of trouble.

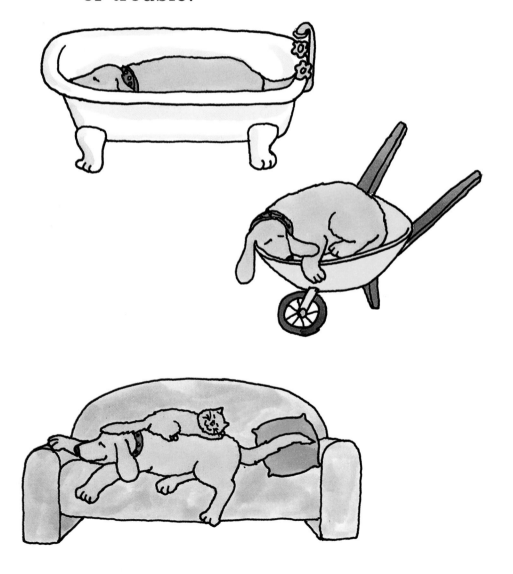

One day, Sam did not have a reason to stay awake. So Sam lay down. He lay down on Mrs. White's rug and went to sleep.

In came Mrs. White. She
wanted to shake the rug.
"Wake up, Sam," she said.
Sam did not wake up. Mrs.
White shook Sam.
"Wake up, you lazy hound
dog," she cried.
Sam did not move.

"Move, Sleepy Sam," shouted
Mrs. White. "I want to shake
the rug."
Sam did not hear Mrs. White.
He did not hear a sound. Sam
was sound asleep.

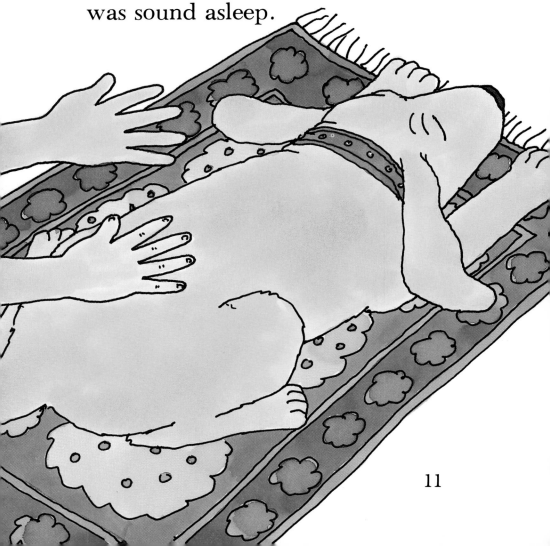

Mrs. White got mad. She moved the rug. She moved the rug with Sam on it. She moved Sam and the rug to the front door.

Mrs. White opened the front
door.
"Out you go, Sleepy Sam," said
Mrs. White.
She pulled the rug. Up it went.
Out the open door went Sleepy
Sam. BUMP!

THUMP! THUMP! THUMP!
Down the front steps rolled
Sleepy Sam. OUCH! Sleepy
Sam was awake now!

14

Mrs. White shook the rug.
Sleepy Sam wanted to go in. He
wanted to go in and sleep.
"Stay out, Sleepy Sam," said
Mrs. White.
And she closed the front door.

"Where now?" thought Sleepy
Sam. "Where can I sleep?"
Sam stopped and smelled.
Bloodhounds like to smell.
Bloodhounds are good at
smelling. Sam smelled something
good. It was something close by.

Sam smelled flowers. He smelled
the flowers in the yard next door.
"What a good smell," thought
Sam.
He went next door.

Sleepy Sam went up to the flowers. There were red flowers. There were white flowers. There were lots of red and white flowers.

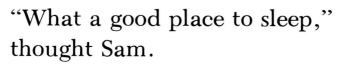

"What a good place to sleep,"
thought Sam.
Where did Sam lie down? He
lay down on the flowers. He
closed his eyes. Oh no, Sleepy
Sam!

Out the front door came Mr.
Day. Down the steps he went.
He went to see his flowers. He
went to see his red and white
flowers. Mr. Day stopped. What
did he see?

"A bloodhound in the flowers!"
he yelled. "Out, Sleepy Sam!
Get out of there!"
Sleepy Sam did not get out. He
rolled over. He rolled on the red
flowers. He rolled on the white
flowers.

Mr. Day got mad. He got so
mad his face got red. His face
got redder than the red flowers.
"No, no, Sleepy Sam," he cried.
"Get out, you bad hound dog."
He pulled Sam.

Sleepy Sam was not a bad hound dog. He was a sleepy hound dog. Sam did not hear Mr. Day. He would not be pulled out. He slept and slept.

"Water," said Mr. Day. "Water
will wake up Sleepy Sam."
So Mr. Day turned on the
sprinkler. He turned the water
on Sam. SPLISH! SPLASH!
SPLOSH!

The water woke Sam up. Hound dogs do not like water. Away ran Sleepy Sam.

Running made Sam dog-tired.
He stopped running. He lay
down. He went to sleep. Sam
went to sleep in a bad place!

The paper boy came by. He
came by on his bike. Sam was
sleeping in a bad place. The
bike could not go by. The paper
boy could not stop.

"Move, Sam, quick!" yelled the
paper boy.
Sam did not hear the paper boy.
He did not hear a sound, and he
did not move.

"Oh no!" cried the paper boy.
He turned his bike. BONK! The
bike fell. OUCH! The paper boy
fell, too.

THUMP! THUMP! THUMP!
The paper boy's papers fell out.
Papers fell here. Papers fell
there. Papers fell everywhere.
What a mess! The paper boy's
face got red. He was mad.
"You made big trouble, Sam,"
he yelled.

Now Sam heard the paper boy.
Sam woke up. Away he ran!

Sam went to Mr. Mack's store.
In his store, Mr. Mack sold eggs.
He sold milk. Mr. Mack sold
eggs and milk and many other
things.

Sam did not have a reason to
stay awake. So he lay down in
front of the store. It was a bad
place to fall asleep. But Sam fell
asleep.

Mrs. White went to Mr. Mack's store. Mrs. White went to buy milk.

Mr. Day went to Mr. Mack's store. Mr. Day went to buy eggs.

Mrs. White came out. She came
out of Mr. Mack's store with
milk. Mr. Day came out. He
came out of Mr. Mack's store
with eggs.

Sam the bloodhound was in a
bad place. Mrs. White did not
see Sam. Mr. Day did not see
Sam. Sleepy Sam did not hear
Mrs. White or Mr. Day.

BUMP! Up went Mrs. White's milk. Down it came. SPLASH! BONK! Up went Mr. Day's eggs. Down they came. SPLOSH! SPLISH!

Eggs and milk were everywhere.
What a mess! Mrs. White
yelled. Mr. Day yelled.
"Wake up, you lazy hound
dog!" they yelled.

Sam did not wake up. He did
not hear the yelling. He did not
hear a sound.

But Mr. Mack heard the sounds.
He heard the yelling.
"What is going on?" he said.
"What is going on in front of
my store?"

Mr. Mack ran out. He ran out
of his store. He ran out quickly.
THUMP! THUMP! THUMP!

42

Mr. Mack did not see Sam.
THUMP! THUMP! THUMP!
He stepped on Sam's tail.

43

OUCH! Sleepy Sam woke up!
OUCH! What a sore tail he had.

Away Sam ran. Away he ran
very quickly. He would not
sleep anywhere anymore.

Now Sam had a reason to stay
awake. It was a good reason.

46

The reason was his tail. A sore tail is a good reason for a bloodhound to stay awake.

Why? Sam did not want his sore tail stepped on anymore. So from that day on, he kept his eyes open.